The Shiny Rose

The Talking Tree

Fyne C. Ogonor

RONVAL INTERNATIONAL
ATLANTA

The Library of Congress has established a Cataloging-in-Publication record for this title.

ISBN
Soft Paper Cover:978-1-951460-44-0
Hard Cover:978-1-951460-42-6
E Book:978-1 951460-43-3

Published in the U.S.A.

Dedication

I dedicate this book, *The Shiny Rose*, to the Creator of the Universe, the Almighty God, who made all things beautiful and lovely.

I further dedicate this book to all educators, and learners of all categories of humanity. Let unity and love prevail.

The Beautiful Garden

Once upon a time, a Shiny Rose was seated in a big tree inside a lovely garden. Visitors often flocked to the garden to admire its beauty, as well as the well-manicured landscape of greenery and other flowers.

The beauty of the Shiny Rose was so pronounced, that the eyes of humans were often drawn to it, so visitors frequently wandered over to the tree to admire the Shiny Rose.

The Rose radiated in daylight, its color reflecting hot pink from the sunshine. At night, the Shiny Rose glowed as if it had its own inherent brilliance that dispelled the darkness around it.

One night, Flower, popularly known as the garden girl in her community, walked to the beautiful tree. She felt drawn by the almost magical lightening of the Shiny Rose.

Flower, the garden girl, was so fascinated that the rose could still be seen clearly and vividly, even in the dark. She touched the Shiny Rose with tender, loving care and asked, "Shiny Rose, what is your secret? Why do humans love you so much? Their faces glow with a smile when they look at you. Even after they visit you, their joyful smile becomes contagious while walking away from you. What is your secret?"

Flower continued, "Could it be your purpose is to be the light in your family? You are the only one that glows at night when it is dark." Finally, Flower added, "I want to be a light in my family like you."

The Shiny Rose answered at once. "Be careful what you wish for! If only you knew my burden, you would feel differently."

"Burden!" Flower exclaimed. "What burden could you have just sitting comfortably on this beautiful tree looking cute? All admire you!"

This time, it was the Green Leaves who answered. "You can say that again! Look at us; we are evergreen. But no one looks at us!

Flower looked at the Green Leaves and smiled sadly. "Green leaves cannot be seen at night because of your color. You are too dark!"

"We are not seen at any time! Every human who walks to this tree only comes to admire the Shiny Rose, just like you! Humans only notice us when they need us for their food or herbs for their health." The Green Leaves were upset, but maybe not as much as The Branches.

"What are you complaining about? At least, occasionally, they appreciate your value. Even if you must end up in their pots and stomachs, they value you! I am the one doing the hardest job and supporting all of you.

Yet, humans only use me to hold on for safety while plucking you, leaves, and fruits. When do they ever admire us?" The Branches asked, tired and disappointed.

But then, the Stem chimed in. "Look who is complaining! Branches, without me, you would not exist at all! They must go through me before they get to you. You do not see me complaining! Instead of admiration, they use their back to lean on me for support. In all, only the Shiny Rose draws humans' admiration."

Hearing all this, the Roots protested. They all talked at once, trying to explain their plight. "Do you know how much effort we put in to keep you all hydrated and constantly nourished?"

One of the Roots made sure they were heard. "You sit up there, showing your beauty to the world, without a word of gratitude to us. Do you know how we feel? Why can't you be grateful for what you have? We are cooped up inside the ground, never beheld by the eyes of humans."

The Green Leaves, however, didn't see it the same way. "You, Roots, are screaming about not being seen by human eyes! What about us? The sun and the rain beat at us regularly. We provide shade for all while you cool off in comfort inside the earth."

A senior Root responded. "If my sibling Roots and I agree to seize the water supply that you need for nourishment, I'd love to see how you will survive."

"We, too, can stop the sun supply for you, and let us see what energy will sustain you."

Suddenly, and to everyone's surprise, the big Taproot spoke up. "Enough! Enough!" She turned to her immediate family, the Roots. "First, you cannot shut down the total supply. If anyone should brag about supplying nourishment to the rest of the family, it is me. You do not see me complaining! I dig deeply into the earth to draw water and other nutrients from the inner world to supply my immediate and extended family members. It is my function as the Creator of heaven and earth and all therein intended. The same applies to every one of you! You have your function, too, to service our existence."

It was silent for a moment, so the Taproot continued. "Remember, we are one family. Cherish each other! We cannot survive without the existence of any of us. We, all parts of a tree, are made for surviving together! None of us can exist without the whole tree body."

Flower, the garden girl, in awe, listened to all the parts as the talking tree argued. She said, "I agree with your elder, the Taproot. It does not matter whether you are inside the ground or out in the open. You are all important. Your coexistence is vital because, as your elder clearly stated, none of you can fully exist without the other parts of the tree. Although each part has its name, you are called a tree together. Complete and whole! And you are beautiful, great to behold by human eyes."

BACK TO HER ROOM

Flower retired to her quarters and remained mesmerized by her experience with the talking tree.

Study

The following day, she went to school as usual. Mrs. Haze, Flower's teacher, asked her class to write an essay on any topic they chose. Without any hesitation, Flower knew precisely what to write about. She smiled to herself and made a note in her notebook.

The Talking Tree
By Flower, the garden girl

A Shiny Rose sits in a big tree inside an attractive garden.

The tree is filled with evergreen leaves.

The stem and branches are soothingly beautiful!

Visitors to the garden never see the hidden roots
responsible for their excellent health and beauty.

The Shiny, bright Rose catches the attention of all visitors
for its beauty.

Everyone walks to the tree to admire the Shiny Rose.

The green leaves wonder! 'Why are they not admiring
us? We are always looking green, healthy, and beautiful,
too.' The green leaves wish to be shiny and bright like the
Shiny Rose, without knowing the burden of the Rose.

The Shiny Rose, in its bud, fears spreading its petals. It fears that the crowd in the garden might touch its soft and fragile petals and diminish her life span.

Let the truth be told: No matter how it tries to delay the spread of its petals, nature's course cannot be changed. Everything in life has a time. You either go with the flow or lose it entirely.

The Rose is beautiful! But her burden is significant. What is there to envy? If only the other parts of the tree realized the truth: The rain falls on all of them. The sun shines on all; even the morning dew has no favorite. The roots are hidden inside the ground, yet they receive the same benefits as the stem, branches, leaves, fruits, and flowers.

The root enjoys the coolness of the earth. Yet, it wishes to be like the other parts above the ground. It regrets not being seen and admired by the people, the visitors of the garden, just like the Shiny Rose.

The stem knows that the branches, leaves, and flowers cannot flourish without them and display their beauty to the world.

The eyes still behold the stem quite often, for it sits at eye level. Why do you envy the fragile flower, the Shiny Rose?

The delectable fruits entice humans who want them for their flavor and nutrition. Still, they wish to be admired like the Shiny Rose.

None of them realize that the Shiny Rose is only so shiny and beautiful because of all of them, who work together, live together, and help each other every day to be one whole.

Live the life you are designed to live. Stop wasting time admiring and wanting to be like the person next to you.

Signed: Flower — the garden girl!

Response

After Flower read her essay to her class, there was silence. Then, Mrs. Haze broke the silence and asked the class, as their customs demanded, if anyone had a question for Flower. The only response she got from her classmates was amazement.

"Wow!" "Incredible!" "Beautiful!" And more displays of astonishment.

In the absence of questions from the students, Mrs. Haze said to Flower, "Your essay has rendered us speechless. It is so relevant that it is mind-blowing. You did a fantastic job!"

"Thank you!" Flower responded.

"Flower, how did you develop the idea in this essay, 'The Talking Tree?'"

Flower smiled. "My father is a gardener, and I spend much time in this garden when I am not in school. So, one night, a shiny light caught my attention, and I walked to the tree to check out the source. Then, I noticed that it was the Shiny Rose glowing like a light. After I initiated a conversation with the Rose, the whole tree started talking to me."

"I see," Mrs. Haze said. "That's a beautiful story. Flower, you have a message for us within your essay. What is the message?"

"Definitely! The talking tree essay is a message to all human beings today."

"Please explain!"

Flower started. "The tree represents humans. For example, let me use our class here. Every one of us is like a part of the tree. Individually, we have our names. We have an elder, you, Mrs. H.! Amongst us are children, boys and girls, all kinds of people. We have future Presidents of Nations and companies here. First Ladies, medical doctors, nurses, teachers like you, Mrs. H, firefighters, scientists, professors, engineers, fashion designers, mechanics, builders, police, homemakers, soldiers, lawyers, preachers, actors, musicians, etc."

She continued. "If all of us here do the same thing, life will not be balanced. It will be too dull and boring. Life is challenging and more interesting because we are all different and have a specific purpose on earth. No matter what our purposes are, they are essential and needed. Hence, we need each other like the tree needs all its parts. Together, we can achieve more and make this world a better and happier planet to live on."

"Like the taproot in my story said, 'We cannot survive without each other.' That also applies to humans. We need all of us to be whole, to live as one body, as our Creator intended for us. There is no need to fight, to feel envy, or to be jealous of each other. We were all born with a specific mission. Let your purpose be your pathway in your life and your journey to your destination. Therefore, focus on walking the trails of life designed only for you in this universe. You are created to be the original 'YOU' the self, and none other! Therefore, live your life to the fullest. Every minute spent wishing and wanting what is not yours is wasted, casting out the excellent life designed for you to enjoy."

She took a deep breath as everyone listened intently. "Be the you that God created! He did not make a mistake with your creation. He made you in His image. That alone should be enough to live a joy-filled and content life. Let your light shine in the world garden like a shiny Rose. Receive the world's admiration, and do not be afraid. Your Creator will not only sustain you, but He will also protect you from all harm. Live with love! Love and enjoy the love that you receive from others. Nothing more will come to you that is not meant to be yours! So, let the love that comes your way not be missed."

The students smiled and clapped. Flower, the garden girl, was as happy as she could be.

THE END

DO NOT HATE! BE KIND AND LOVE ONE ANOTHER.

"Let everything you do be done in love"

1 Corinthians 16: 14 (AMP).

Other books
by the author

About the Author

Fyne Ogonor is an Educator, Entrepreneur, inspirational and motivational Speaker, Philanthropist, Business Consultant, Author, Songwriter, and Spiritual Counselor.

Her other books include *Baby Eagle and the Chicks series, The Best Gift Ever, A Moving Train, My Pledge! The Power of Prayer and Discover Your Coat of Many Colors: You Were Born to be Significant.*